This one is dedicated to my daughters Briana and Shana.
Without you there wouldn't have been an inspiration for writing children's books.
You make being a dad fun. I love you both.

To: Roman
May reading always remain
Special.
All the best,
David Roth
2018

We're tired and worn out, we just need to rest
We gave it our all now, we gave it our best
Our family visit is just now winding down
From a week long vacation with grandpa in town

I'll tell you, I'm glad to just sit and relax
My sisters and I lying flat on our backs
And we didn't expect it, there was no way of knowing
Just what all can happen when grandpa gets going

From the moment he got here he wanted to play

He wrestled and tickled and chased us all day

He swung us around and we bounced on his knee

Then he helped us pick apples that grew on our tree

That first night he waited to tuck us
   in bed

And then several stories for bedtime
   he read

He kissed us goodnight in our room
   where we'd lay

Then he woke us up early the very
   next day

The sun wasn't up and the room was still dark

But grandpa was waiting to go to the park

He told us to hurry and get ourselves dressed

We ate quick then left with our hair all a mess

Each day his car seats would be filled
   with fun stuff

He would pack quite a lot, there'd be
   more than enough

He had fishing gear, grasshoppers,
   worms and a net

He had even packed raincoats in case
   we got wet

There were horseshoes and Frisbees,
some board games and cards

There were helmets and roller blades
too with shin guards

We knew then, once it started, there'd
be no chance of slowing

Or how long it will all last, when
grandpa gets going

When we fished with our grandpa
we learned to duck fast

So we wouldn't get caught on his
hook when he'd cast

He would tell wild stories about
when he was young

And he taught us to whistle and
sing songs he'd sung

He would always keep up with
the latest of trends

And loved showing us off to most
all of his friends

He liked rock and roll music and
video games

And met real famous singers and
actors he claims

He bought us ice cream with
    all the toppings in sight

He filled water balloons up
    and started the fight

We would order spaghetti and
    eat with a slurp

Then we'd all have a contest
    and give our best burp

He would save all his pennies
and bring them to share

Then outside he would throw
them all up in the air

He said not to tell grandma, it'd be best her not knowing

'Cause when she comes a chasin' he'd just best keep going

And that's what he did so he found a parade

And we got front row seats, by the street, in the shade

But when that got too crowded and too hard to see

Why that grandpa of ours found us seats in a tree

And that's where we stayed 'till the
crowd disappeared

Playing games taking turns making
faces all weird

Then onward we went playing tag
down the street

We took off our shoes and he tickled
our feet

We went to the circus, th
 park and the pool

We played in the sun wit
 a hose to keep cool

One day he bought snow
 cones and then we
 rode bikes

Another we'd play in the
 fields on our hikes

There wasn't a moment he'd
 just let go by

We didn't have time to get
 bored or just sigh

And we could not have guessed,
 there was no way of
 knowing

Just what would all happen,
 when grandpa gets going?

So what did he do when we'd come
    home each night?

And where would he go once he's
    turned out our light?

Well I wasn't quite sure just what all
    he had done

But he did quite a lot before morning
    would come

When grandpa gets going, the coffee starts perking
The stories get told and the monsters start lurking
The sprinklers starts sprinkling, the mower starts mowing
The bushes get trimmed and the garden starts growing
The horseshoes get thrown and the dust all gets flying
The fish will get scared by the flies he'll be tying
The car will be warm and the wheels will be turning
The cake will be made and ice cream will be churning
The tools will be tooling, the wood will be stacked
The saws will be sawing, the gear will be packed
The cards will be shuffled, the chairs will be rocking
The house will be busy and the town will be talking
The tickets will be bought, the bills will be paid
The fun will all happen, 'cause the plans will be made
There's just one thing for sure you can bet without knowing
There's no end to the party, when grandpa gets going

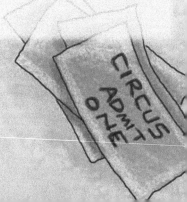

But then...

On the last day while racing him
    home to the door

We all went inside and fell flat on
    the floor

We couldn't believe all the things
    we had done

He had packed, in a week, a whole
    year full of fun

But grandpa, he wandered back out
    to the lawn

We watched as he put both his hat
    and coat on

So I lifted my head to the window to
    see

Just where he had gone to, now
    where could he be?

And what I saw next, well, it
    made me quite sad

My grandpa and grandma were
    with mom and dad

And they had all their luggage,
    they were ready to leave

My mouth fell wide open, I
    could not believe

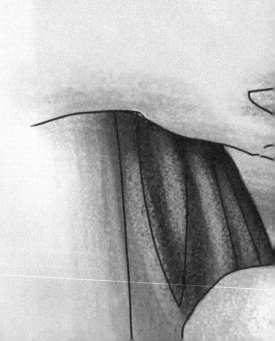

My sisters and I quickly ran out the
  door

We all had to hug him and kiss him
  once more

We clung to him tightly with a tear
  and a sigh

He smiled at us gently and winked
  with his eye

I'd never felt breathless or choked up before

And I blinked away tears as he closed the car door

But we all knew right then, it's a time well worth knowing

We'll grow up with fond memories of when grandpa gets going

The end... but not really

David Radman is an award-winning author who began writing children's stories as a single father, when his two daughters were very young. His love of being a dad inspired him to share his creativity through the magic of storytelling. He continues to write stories he hopes to share in the future. David lives in Littleton, Colorado with his wife Michelle, and children. This is his second book.

Douglas Shuler has been drawing and painting for as long as he can remember. Classically trained in traditional art mediums, he transitioned to digital methods and can create imagery using most any technique, from whimsical cartoons to professional portraiture. He has a passion for science fiction and fantasy illustration and has worked on everything from book covers to comic books, from video games to television concept art. Internationally published, he is best known for his fantasy illustrations that appear in the popular trading card game, *Magic: The Gathering*.

This is a work of fiction. Names, characters, businesses, places,
events and incidents are either the products of the author's imagination
or used in a fictitious manner. Any resemblance to actual persons,
living or dead, or actual events is purely coincidental.

ISBN: 978-1-61296-999-2
PUBLISHED BY BLACK ROSE WRITING
www.blackrosewriting.com

Printed in the United States of America
Suggested Retail Price (SRP) $14.95

When Grandpa Gets Going is printed in Times New Roman

CPSIA information can be obtained
at www.ICGtesting.com
Printed in the USA
LVHW01s1910010218
564967LV00003B/3/P